The Sand
Dragon

L

D1152086

30118131876264

READZ●NE
ReadZone Books Limited

First published in this edition 2015

© in this edition ReadZone Books Limited 2015
© in text Su Swallow 2005
© in illustrations Silvia Raga 2005

Su Swallow has asserted her right under the Copyright Designs
and Patents Act 1988 to be identified as the author of this work.

Silvia Raga has asserted her right under the Copyright Designs
and Patents Act 1988 to be identified as the illustrator of this work.

Every attempt has been made by the Publisher to secure appropriate
permissions for material reproduced in this book. If there has been any
oversight we will be happy to rectify the situation in future editions or
reprints. Written submissions should be made to the Publisher.

British Library Cataloguing in Publication Data (CIP) is available
for this title.

Printed in Malta by Melita Press.

All rights reserved. No part of this publication may be reproduced,
stored in a retrieval system or transmitted, in any form or by any
means, electronic, mechanical, photocopying, recording or otherwise,
without the prior permission of ReadZone Books Limited.

ISBN 978 1 78322 127 1

Visit our website: www.readzonebooks.com

The Sand Dragon

Su Swallow
and Silvia Raga

Lancashire Library Services	
30118131876264	
PETERS	JF
£5.99	12-Oct-2015
SEU 10|15.	

The seaside!

Splish splash!

7

Look!

Hurray!

10

"What's that?" said Mum.

"A sand dragon."
They both went home.

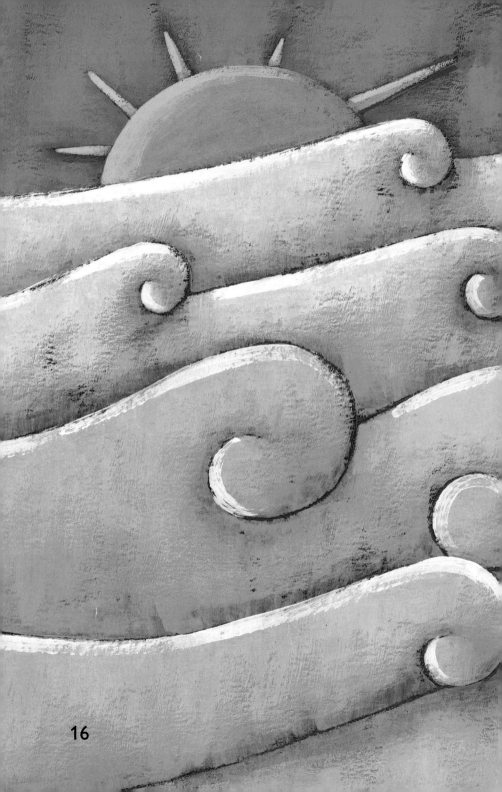

16

The waves splashed,

17

the dragon swam,

19

and nibbled,

and danced.

The waves moved back.

24

The dragon lay on the
sand to dry.

Edward came back.

28

"Mummy, my sand dragon
hasn't moved all night!"

Did you enjoy this book?

Look out for more *Robins* titles –
first stories in only 50 words

A Head Full of Stories by Su Swallow and Tim Archbold
ISBN 978 1 78322 456 2

Billy on the Ball by Paul Harrison and Silvia Raga
ISBN 978 1 78322 125 7

Countdown! by Kay Woodward and Ofra Amit
ISBN 978 1 78322 462 3

Cave-Baby and the Mammoth by Vivian French and Lisa Williams
ISBN 978 1 78322 126 4

Hattie the Dancing Hippo by Jillian Powell and Emma Dodson
ISBN 978 1 78322 463 0

Molly is New by Nick Turpin and Silvia Raga
ISBN 978 1 78322 455 5

Mr Bickle and the Ghost by Stella Gurney and Silvia Raga
ISBN 978 1 78322 472 2

Noisy Books by Paul Harrison and Fabiano Fiorin
ISBN 978 1 78322 464 7

Not-So-Silly Sausage by Stella Gurney and Liz Million
ISBN 978 1 78322 465 4

The Sand Dragon by Su Swallow and Silvia Raga
ISBN 978 1 78322 127 1

Undersea Adventure by Paul Harrison and Barbara Nascimbeni
ISBN 978 1 78322 466 1

Yummy Scrummy by Paul Harrison and Belinda Worsley
ISBN 978 1 78322 467 8